TORI AMOS
LYRICS

OMNIBUS PRESS
LONDON · NEW YORK · SYDNEY

Many thanks to Edison and Mary Ellen Amos
and to
Billy Reckert
for their kind and invaluable assistance.

Illustrated by Herb Leonhard

Published 2001 by Omnibus Press
A Division of Music Sales Coporation, New York

Hardcover Edition
Order No. OP 48521
US ISBN: 0.8256.1887.8
UK ISBN: 0.7119.8982.6

Softcover Edition
Order No. OP 48131
US ISBN: 0.8256.1692.1
UK ISBN: 0.7119.7626.0

Exclusive Distributors:
Music Sales Corporation
257 Park Avenue South
New York City, NY 10010, USA

Music Sales Limited,
8/9 Frith Street,
London W1V 5TZ, UK

Music Sales PTY, Ltd
120 Rothschild Avenue
Roseberry, NSW 2018
Australia

Printed in the United States of America by Vicks Lithograph and Printing Corp.

TABLE OF CONTENTS

Foreword

the songs are alive. they sleep sometimes, but they are very much alive. I guess knowing that they are all souls that have just chosen to form in the structure of a song has kept me from ever feeling truly alone in this world. also the concept of death and where do we go when we leave this place??? it has always fascinated me that no matter what technology we have access to, we cannot begin to locate our loved ones once they leave the planet. where do souls go when they die…[no one can answer that definitively but we know we are drawn to people and places and these people and places seem familiar]. knowing that the next time I run into my mother, I won't have any recollection of this life, there won't be a photo album—the times we played hopscotch, shared cuddles, tears—when everything went wrong she was there to hold me…what she is and was to me, and I won't know her as 'mother,' but I believe I will be drawn to her, whatever form she takes or I take…am I mother of these songs? on some level, yes. they are pieces of me, but I guess there is a piece of my mother in me, as it seems there is a small piece of me in my daughter Natashya. the songs. they teach me. do you remember ever playing with a prism??? every time you hold it differently in the light, you find a whole new world. sound.

that is a world. wow. the ancient Egyptians believed in the power of the tone. the tone of a word. so, not just the definition of the word, as in Webster's, but the resonance, the bloodline of the word. combinations of words bring up pictures...with song lyrics, I always try and pull back and see how the word makes me feel...languid, covert, direct, coded, honeysuckle, roses, wood, horses, sweat, stale—these words are universes—we could follow the family tree of a word, like we could follow a ski trail down a mountain, there are offshoots—some get harder to traverse, there are obstacles to overcome, there are challenges. a word can blow open doors that you didn't know were trapdoors in the floor. so o.k. death—actually an easy one, I think. that particular subject is so rich and is at the core of our internal questioning—whereas saying the wrong thing to someone—misunderstandings, how to express that in a song, writing 'saying the wrong thing' right now that's tricky. when you say that thing that starts an argument, and have no idea—how did you offend this person that you really really like...and you can't take it back. words are like guns. they do wound...as we all know. sometimes I truly believe it's the space between the words that matters. as some would say, the way you say a word and what you pair it with—changes its meaning. that's when the magic happens, when the combination of words and tone hit a bull's eye from your kundalini chakra through your heart chakra—shocks your circuits and is able to converse with your unconscious—where so many stored sleeping parts of oneself hibernate. that is probably the thing you are hunting for as a writer, the way in through the prism. hunting. word and tone hunters, tracking the perfume of a word and a sound. sometimes the pairing seems illicit, sometimes it causes friction, but when it works, it makes one's body respond in some way. a lyric book is only part of who these girls are because they all have sound with them as their subtext. whereas poetry does not have music, music is its own language and the two go hand in hand. I hope you enjoy this layer of the cake.

as always

tori.

AGENT ORANGE

gotta tell you
what I heard from Agent Orange
Mister Suntan
Mister Happy Man
Mister I know the girls on all the world tours
Mister Agent
he's my favourite
and they don't understand
he's got palm oil fans
yes he's down
and there
and everywhere
he's getting an A to Z
an underwater city
where she swims and swims

Alamo

alamo
heard all about your fandango
banged on my knees on your back door
only to wake you to blues on the way
blues on the way
blues on the way

embarcar
figures you'll see me as older
twenty-three hours till the border
don't think I'll be going as fast as I came
fast as I came
fast as I came

tears on my pillow
of course they're not mine
alter that altar
making a play
somebody invent the telephone line
I'll take mine
my chances

alamo
wish I could do what gold does
heard that the stars were in order
got yourself dealt a hand with
two queen of spades
and blues on the way
blues on the way

tears on my pillow
of course they're not mine
alter that altar
making a play
somebody, just somebody, invent the telephone line
I'll take my chances

BACHELORETTE

bachelorette you climb on rooftops and you bachelorette
you can turn dust into champagne
you even remembered his name

bachelorette, the braves you painted pink for bachelorettes
you tried to show him that he can
but you can never rush a man

you must remember
you're a car girl
you're a star girl
you are at the door
the tide will turn
there's a window

bachelorette the things you do girls
to your bachelorettes...
you thought that...

you must remember
you're a car girl
you're a star girl
you are at the door
the tide will turn
there's a window

bachelorette, you fly alone now and you cry sometimes
there's nothing like it in the world
you'll go to Paris on your own
just bachelorette you climb on rooftops and you bachelorette
you can turn dust into champagne
you even yidiedididi...

Baker Baker

Baker Baker baking a cake make me a day make me whole again and I wonder what's in a day what's in your cake this time

I guess you heard he's gone to L.A. he says that behind my eyes I'm hiding and he tells me I pushed him away that my heart's been hard to find

here there must be something here there must be something here here

Baker Baker can you explain if truly his heart was made of icing and I wonder how mine could taste maybe we could change his mind

I know you're late for your next parade you came to make sure that I'm not running well I ran from him in all kinds of ways guess it was his turn this time

time thought I'd made friends with time thought we'd be flying maybe not this time

Baker Baker baking a cake make me a day make me whole again and I wonder if he's ok if you see him say hi

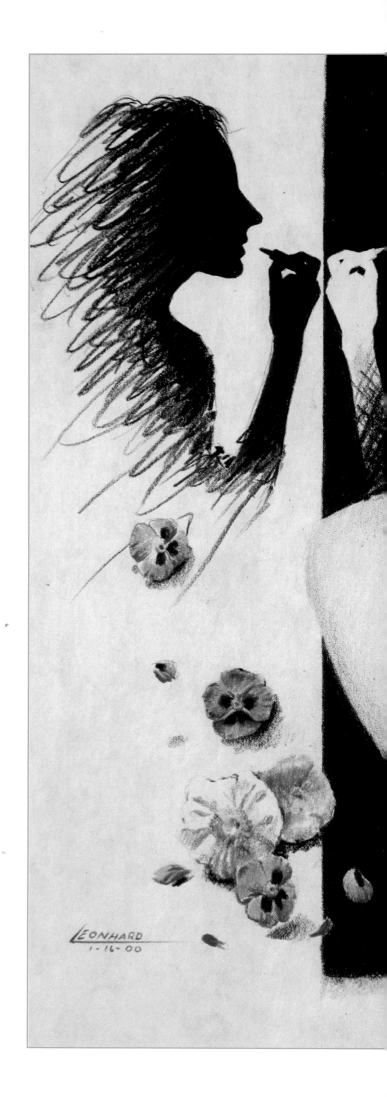

BEAUTY QUEEN

She's a Beauty Queen
my sweet bean bag in the street
take it
down out to the laundry scene
don't know why she's in my hand
can't figure what it is
but I lie again

Bells for Her

and through the life force and there goes her friend on her Nishiki it's out of time and through the portal they can make amends

hey would you say whatever we're blanket friends can't stop what's coming can't stop what is on its way

and through the walls they made their mudpies I've got your mind I said she said I've your voice I said you don't need my voice girl you have your own but you never thought it was enough of so they went years and years like sisters blanket girls always there through that and this there's nothing we cannot ever fix I said

can't stop what's coming can't stop what is on its way Bells and footfalls and soldiers and dolls brothers and lovers she and I were now she seems to be sand under his shoes there's nothing I can do can't stop what's coming can't stop what is on its way

and now I speak to you are you in there you have her face and her eyes but you are not her and we go at each other like blank ettes who can't find their thread and their bare

can't stop loving can't stop what is on its way and I see it coming and it's on its way

Beulah land

beulah land
got a wasted gun
licorice man
I'll sum you up thumbs up
got something in that sand
beulah girl
you been hitchin me up

got some candy
and a sweet sing
give me religion
and a lobotomy

beulah land
you beautiful whore
tell me when
I don't need you anymore

said that somewhere
you're gonna get something here
so you're right in the middle
and then I'm you
something is coming back again
I said
you
maybe I don't wanna go
to where you're not, and so

beulah land
gonna find me a worm
a place to bathe this body on down
got a rubber board
and a crocodile
gonna float
on past your home
say when
just say when
just say when

BLACK SWAN

Ride on, ride on friends of the black swan
ride on, ride on do you know where she's gone
gumdrops and Saturdays did Eric call by the way
he knew, he knew, and he knew where the pillow goes

ride on, ride on friends of the black swan
ride on, ride on do you know where she's gone
buttercups and fishing flies the biggest thickest ever sky
I know they know something
I know

ride on, ride on now friends of the black swan
ride on, ride on you know where she's gone

little green men do O.K.
it's the fairies' revenge they say
and gumdrops and Saturdays did Eric call by the way

ride on, ride on, ride on

BLACK-DOVE (JANUARY)

she was a january girl
she never let on how insane it was
in that tiny kinda scary house
by the woods
by the woods
by the woods
black-dove black-dove
you're not a helicopter
you're not a cop out either
black-dove black-dove
you don't need a space ship
they don't know you've already lived
on the other side of the galaxy
she had a january world
so many storms not right somehow
how a lion becomes a mouse
by the woods
but I have to get to TEXAS
said I have to get to TEXAS
and I'll give away my blue blue dress
she has a january girl
she never let on how insane it was
in that tiny kinda scary house
by the woods

Bliss

Father, I killed my monkey »»»
I let it out to »»» taste the
sweet of spring »»» wonder if
I will wander out »»» test my
tether to »»» see if I'm still free
»»» from you

steady as it comes »»» right
down »»» to you »»» I've said it
all »»» so maybe we're a Bliss
»»» of another kind

lately, I'm in to circuitry »»»
what it means to be »»» made
of you but not enough for you
»»» and I wonder if »»» you
can bilocate is that »»» what I
taste »»» your supernova juice
»»» you know it's true I'm part
of you

steady as it comes »»» right
down to you »»» I've said it all
»»» so maybe you're a 4 horse
engine »»» with a power drive
»»» a hot kachina who wants
into mine »»» take it with your
terracide »»» we're a Bliss »»»
of another kind

BLOOD ROSES

Blood Roses
Blood Roses
Back on the street now
can't forget the things you never said
on days like these starts me thinking
when chickens get a taste of your meat
chickens get a taste of your meat

you gave him your blood
and your warm little diamond
he likes killing you after you're dead
you think I'm a queer
I think you're a queer
I think you're a queer
Said I think you're a queer
and I shaved every place where you been
I shaved every place where you been

God knows I know I've thrown away those graces

the Belle of New Orleans tried to show me
once how to tango
wrapped around your feet
wrapped around like good little roses

Blood Roses
Blood Roses
back on the street now
now you've cut out the flute
from the throat of the loon
at least when you cry now
he can't even hear you
when chickens get a taste of your meat
when he sucks you deep
sometimes you're nothing but meat

BUTTERFLY

Stinky soul get a little lost in my own
Hey General, need a little love in that hole of yours
one ways, now, and Saturdays and our kittens all wrapped in cement
from cradle to gundrops
got me running girl as fast as I can
and is it right Butterfly they like you better framed and dried

Daddy dear if I can kill one man why not two
well, nurses smile when you got iron veins
you can't stain their pretty shoes and pom poms and cherry blondes
and their kittens still wrapped in cement
from God's saviors to gundrops
got me running girl as fast as I can
and is it right Butterfly they like you better framed and dried

got a pretty pretty garden pretty garden yes
got me a pretty pretty garden a pretty garden yes
got me a pretty pretty garden a pretty garden

Caught a Lite Sneeze

Caught a lite sneeze caught a lite breeze
caught a lightweight lightningseed
boys on my left side
boys on my right side

boys in the middle
and you're not here I need a big loan
from the girl zone

building
tumbling down
didn't know our love was so small
couldn't stand at all
Mr St. John just bring your son

the spire is hot
and my cells can't feed
and you still got that Belle dragging your foots
I'm hiding it well Sister Ernestine
but I still got that Belle
dragging my foots

right on time you get closer
and closer
called my name but there's no way in
use that fame
rent your wife and kids today
maybe she will
maybe she will caught a lite sneeze
dreamed a little dream
made my own pretty hate machine
boys on my left side
boys on my right side
boys in the middle and you're not here
boys in their dresses
and you're not here
I need a big loan from the girl zone

CHINA

CHINA all the way to New York I can feel the distance getting close you're right next to me but I need an airplane I can feel the DISTANCE as you breathe *sometimes I think you want me to touch you how can I when you build the great WALL around you in your eyes I saw a future together you just look away in the distance* china decorates our table funny how the CRACKS don't seem to show pour the wine dear you say we'll take a holiday but we never can agree on where to go China all the way to New York maybe you got lost in MEXICO you're right next to me I think that you can hear me funny how the distance learns to grow I can feel the distance I can feel the distance I can feel the distance getting close

CLOUD ON MY TONGUE

Someone's knockin on my kitchen door leave the wood outside what all the girls here are freezing cold leave me with your Borneo I don't need much to keep me warm

don't stop now what you're doin my ugly one Bring them all here
hard to hide a hundred girls in your hair it won't be fair if I hate her if I ate her you can go now

You're already in there I'll be wearing your tattoo you're already in there

Got a cloud sleeping on my tongue he goes then it goes and kiss the violets as they're waking up

Leave me with your Borneo leave me the way I was before

You're already in there I'll be wearing your tattoo I'm already in circles and circles and circles again the girl's in circles and circles got to stop spinning circles and circles and circles again thought I was over the bridge now

Concertina

clouds descending I'm not
policing what you think and
dream I run into your thought
from across the room just
another trick can I weather
this I've got a fever above my
waist you got a squeeze box
on your knee I know the truth
is in between the 1st and the
40th drink concertina
concertina a chill that bends
this I swear you're the fiercest
calm I've been in concertina
concertina try infrared this I
swear you're the fiercest calm
I've been in the soul-quake
happened here in a glass
world particle by particle she
slowly changes she likes
hanging chinese paper cuts
just another fix can I weather
this I got my fuzz all tipped to
play I got a dub on your
landscape then there's your
policy of trancing the sauce
without the blame too far too
far too far it could all get way
too cheerful concertina I know
the truth lies in between the
1st and the 40th drink clouds
descending

Cooling

maybe I didn't like to hear
but I still can't believe Speed Racer is dead
so then I thought I'd make some plans
but Fire thought she'd really rather be Water instead

and Peggy got a message for me, from Jesus
and I heard every word that you have said
and I know I have been driven like the snow
but this is cooling
faster than I can
this is cooling
faster than I

so then Love walked up to Like
said I know that you don't like me much
let's go for a ride
this ocean is wrapped around that pineapple tree
and is your place in heaven worth giving up these kisses these yes these kisses

and Peggy got a message for me, from Jesus
and I heard every word that you have said
and I know I have been driven like the snow
but this is cooling
faster than I can
this is cooling
faster than I
this is cooling
this is cooling
this is cool cooling
this is cooling

Cool on Your island

if you don't treat me better
baby I'll just run away
baby I don't know what drives you
to play all these silly games
c'mon baby
I'm much stronger than you know
sometimes
I'm not afraid
to let it show

when will you wake up
I want you more than the stars
and the sun
but I can take only so much
cool on your island
is it cool on your island

I got a brand new dress babe
could it make you wanna try
I guess I didn't want to notice
the stars gone
from your eyes
c'mon baby
I'm much stronger than you know
sometimes
I'm not afraid
to let it show

when will you wake up
I want you more than the stars
and the sun
but I can take only so much
cool on your island
is it cool on your island

we could buy an airplane
build a home in the sand
you could tell your secrets
I could understand
but then by the morning
comes crumblin' down
and as your leavin'
wait

when will you wake up
I want you more than the stars
and the sun
but I can take only so much
cool on your island
you're so cool on your island
is it cool on your island

if you don't treat me better
baby I'll just run away
if you don't treat me
one day
you'll wake up cold
then you'll know
you'll know
you'll know
you love me

CORNFLAKE GIRL

Never was a cornflake girl thought that was a good solution hangin with the raisin girls she's gone to the other side givin us a yo heave ho things are getting kind of gross and I go at sleepy time this is not really happening you bet your life it is

Peel out the watchword just peel out the watchword

She knows what's goin on seems we got a cheaper feel now all the sweeteaze are gone gone to the other side with my encyclopedia they musta paid her a nice price she's puttin on her string bean love this is not really happening you bet your life it is

Rabbit where'd you put the keys girl and the man with the golden gun thinks he knows so much Rabbit where'd you put the keys girl

CRUCIFY

every finger in the room is pointing at me I wanna spit in their faces then I get afraid of what that could bring I got a bowling ball in my stomach I got a desert in my mouth figures that my COURAGE would choose to sell out now I've been looking for a savior in these dirty streets looking for a savior beneath these dirty sheets I've been raising up my hands drive another nail in just what GOD needs one more victim *why do we crucify ourselves every day I crucify myself nothing I do is good enough for you crucify myself every day and my HEART is sick of being in chains* got a kick for a dog beggin' for LOVE I gotta have my suffering so that I can have my cross I know a cat named Easter he says will you ever learn you're just an empty cage girl if you kill the bird I've been looking for a savior in these dirty streets looking for a savior beneath these dirty sheets I've been raising up my hands drive another nail in got enough GUILT to start my own religion please be save me I CRY

CRUEL

so don't give me respect don't give me a piece of your preciousness
flaunt all she's got in our old neighbourhood I'm sure she'll make a few friends
even the rain bows down let us pray as you cock-cock-cock your mane
no cigarettes only peeled HAVANAS for you I can be cruel
I don't know why
why can't my ba.ll.oo.n stay up in a perfectly windy sky
I can be cruel I don't know why
dance with the Sufis celebrate your top ten in the charts of pain
lover brother bogenvilla my vine twists around your need
even the rain is sharp like today as you sh-sh-shock me sane
no cigarettes only peeled HAVANAS for you I can be cruel

Daisy Dead Petals

Daisy Dead Petals that is her name
she's in a phone booth phase so
underneath the shade of a peppermint tray
she can turn it out with a heal on she just rides into town
knowing what they'll say knowing they're around the corner
got a crack in got a crack in some strange places

Daisy Dead Petals that is her name.
so maybe she tastes like a hamburger maid well
these dead petals honey brought me here
she said "these dead petals honey brought me here"

dancing on a dime hearing mother cry
maybe she's around the corner

got a crack in got a crack in some strange places
on my back with on my back with some dirty dishes

falling down, falling down, all over the river
falling down, falling down, falling down

wish what I'm feeling could go on like this forever
falling down, falling down, falling down

and since we're down might as well stay
might as well fry some eggs
and wave to the shade of the peppermint tray
she's a new friend not a skeleton to ride into town
knowing what they'll say knowing she tastes like a hamburger maid, but

"these dead petals honey brought me here"
she said, "these dead petals honey brought me here"

Dātura

get out of my garden

passion vine
texas sage
indigo spires salvia
confederate jasmine
royal cape plumbago
arica palm
pygmy date palm
snow-on-the-mountain
pink powderpuff
Dātura
crinum lily
st. christopher's lily
silver dollar eucalyptus
white african iris
katie's charm ruellia
variegated shell ginger
florida coontie
Dātura
ming fern
sword fern
dianella
walking iris
chocolate cherries allamanda
awabuki viburnum

is there room in my heart
for you to follow your heart
and not need more blood
from the tip of your star

walking iris
chocolate cherries allamanda
awabuki viburnun

natal plum
black magic ti
mexican bush sage
gumbo limbo
golden shrimp
belize shrimp
senna
weeping sabicu
golden shower tree
golden trumpet tree
bird of paradise
come in
variegated shell ginger
Dātura
lonicera
red velvet costus
xanadu philodendron
snow queen hibiscus
frangipani
bleeding heart
persian shield
cat's whiskers
royal palm
sweet alyssum
petting bamboo
orange jasmine
clitoria blue pea
downy jasmine
Dātura
frangipani

dividing Canaan
piece by piece
o let me see
dividing Canaan

Doughnut Song

had me a trick and a kick and your message
well you'll never gain weight from a doughnut hole
then thought that I could decipher your message
there's no one here dear
no one at all

and if I'm wasting all your time
this time
maybe you never learned to take
and if I'm hanging on to your shade
I guess I'm way beyond the pale

and southern men can grow gold
can grow pertty
blood can be pertty
like a delicate man
copper to steel to a hinge that is faltered
that lets you in lets you in lets you in
something's just keeping you numb

you told me last night
you were a sun now with your very own

devoted satellite
happy for you
and I am sure that I hate you
two sons too many too many able fires

and if I'm wasting all your time
this time
I think you never learned to take
and if I'm hanging on to your shade
I guess I'm way beyond the pale

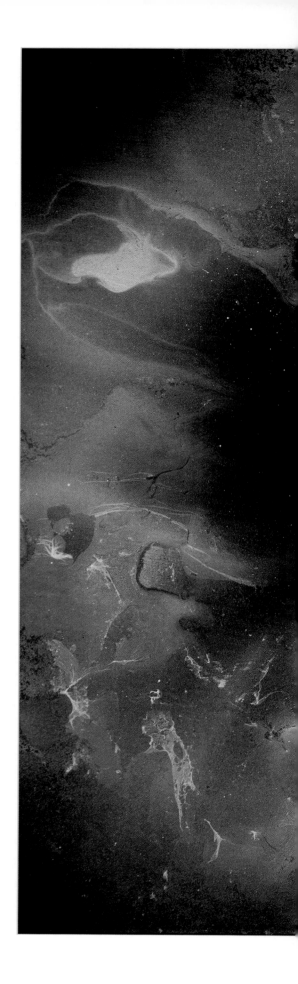

ETIENNE

Maybe I'm a witch lost in time
running through the fields of Scotland by your side
kicked out of France but I still believe
taken to a land far across the sea

Etienne, Etienne
hear the west wind whisper my name
Etienne, Etienne
by the morning maybe we'll remember who I am

maybe you're the knight who saved my life
maybe we faced the fire side by side
here we are again under the same sky
as the gypsy crystal slowly dies

Etienne, Etienne
hear the west wind whisper my name
Etienne, Etienne
by the morning maybe we'll remember who I am

I close my eyes see you again
I know I've held you but I can't remember where or when

Etienne, Etienne
hear the west wind whisper my name
Etienne, Etienne
by the morning maybe we'll remember who I am

maybe I'm a witch

FATHER LUCIFER

Father Lucifer
you never looked so sane
you always did prefer the drizzle to the rain
tell me that you're still in love with that Milkmaid
how's the Lizzies
how's your Jesus Christ been hanging

nothings gonna stop me from floating
nothings gonna stop me from floating

he says he reckons I'm a watercolour stain
he says I run and then I run from him
and then I run
he didn't see me watching
from the aeroplane
he wiped a tear
and then he threw away our appleseed

nothings gonna stop me from floating

everyday's my wedding day
though baby's still in his comatose state
I'll die my own Easter eggs
don't go yet
and Beenie lost the sunset but that's OK
does Joe bring flowers to Marilyn's grave
and girls that eat pizza and never gain weight
Father Lucifer you never looked so sane

FLOATING CITY

You went away
why did you leave me
you know I believed you
nothing explained
where are the answers
I know I need you
tell me is your city paved with gold
is there hunger
do your people grow old
do your governments have secrets that they've sold

every night I wait take me away
to your floating city
by my window at night
I see the lights to your floating city
come and take me away
I want to play in your floating city
floating city

T.V. turns off
any of us that
say that we've seen you
tell me are we
the only planet
that can't conceive you
will we be like Atlantis long ago
so assured that we're advanced
with what we know
that our spirit never had time to grow

is it weak to look for
saviors out in space
little Earth she tries so hard
to change our ways
sometimes she must get
sick of this place

FLYING DUTCHMAN

Hey kid, I got a ride for you
they say your brain is a comic book tattoo
and you'll never be anything
what will you do with your life
that's all you hear from noon till night

take a trip on a rocket ship baby where the sea is the sky
I know the guy who runs the place and he's out-a-sight
Flying Dutchman are you out there
Flying Dutchman are you out there

straight suits, they don't understand
she tried, that one, with the alligator boots but the other side drew her in
heart falling fast when she left, even the Milky Way was dressed in black

take a trip on a rocket ship baby where the sea is the sky
I know the guy who runs the place and he's out-a-sight
Flying Dutchman are you out there
Flying Dutchman are you out there

cause they can't see what you're born to be
they can see me
they can't be
what they can't believe
they can see what you see

they'll keep the boy spinning in their own little world ah.
tie him up so he won't say a word
they'll keep the boy spinning in their own little world
so afraid he'll be what they never were

FROG ON MY TOE

Papa I know
there's a frog on my toe
maybe I'll call him Jethro
maybe I'll grow up to be wise, as good as he
and maybe I'll come back after you're long gone

Papa I'm sure
the worms have eaten you now
and Jethro's been on some Frenchy's plate long ago
now I'm pretty sure that I listen to every word
'cause I still hear you telling me still

slap them boys when they're naughty
make them crawl, make you haughty
make you strong, little girl
you paint them toes the reddest color
and you know one day
you're gonna be bigger than a flea
you're gonna be bigger than that old poison ivy tree

now I'm pretty sure
that I think you'd come and visit
and talk sometimes kinda like Gidget
a funny little chance like an Indian Brave
you said, "we all grew fat when the white man came"
but one day, girl, you're gonna learn to make 'em crawl
make 'em grow tall
but have the grace
to be a lady with disgrace
and you fry them taters
and you make them with lady's hands
and know you're my pappy's baby

Girl

from in the shadow she calls in and in the shadow she finds a way finds a way and in the shadow she CRAWLS clutching her faded photograph my IMAGE under her thumb yes with a message for my heart yes with a message for my heart *she's been everybody else's girl maybe one day she'll be her own everybody else's girl maybe one day she'll be her own* and in the doorway they stay and laugh as violins fill with water screams from the BLUEBELLS can't make them go away we'll I'm not seventeen but I've cuts on my knees falling down as the winter takes one more CHERRY TREE rushin' rivers thread so thin limitations dream with the flying pigs turbid blue and the drugstores too safe in their coats anda in their do's yeah smother in our hearts a pillow to my dots *one day maybe one day one day she'll be her own* and in the mist there she rides and castles are burning in my heart and as I twist I hold tight and I ride to work every morning wondering why "sit in the chair and be good now" and become all that they told you the white coats enter her room and I'm callin' my baby callin' my baby callin' my baby callin' *everybody else's girl maybe one day she'll be her own*

GOD

God sometimes you just don't come through God sometimes you just don't come through do you need a woman to look after you God sometimes you just don't come through

You make pretty daisies pretty daisies love I gotta find what you're doing about things here a few witches burning gets a little toasty here I gotta find why you always go when the wind blows tell me you're crazy maybe then I'll understand you got your 9 iron in the back seat just in case heard you've gone south well babe you love your new 4 wheel I gotta find why you always go when the wind blows

Will you even tell her if you decide to make the sky fall will you even tell her if you decide to make the sky

GLORY OF THE 80's

I took a taxi from LA to Venus »» in 1985 I was electromagnetically sucked »» back into a party going on that night »» It was the glory of the 80's »» with karma drawn up in lines »» and two bugle boy models saying 'baby, »» it's a freebee you sure look deprived' »» I had the Story of O in my bucket seat »» of my wanna be Mustang »» auditioning for reptiles in their »» Raquel Welsh campaign »» in the glories of the 80's »» you said "I'm not afraid to die" »» I said I don't find that remotely »» funny even on this space cake high »» and then when it all seemed clear »» just then you go and disappear »» silicone party barbies to the left and »» Joan of Arcs to the right »» no one feeling insecure we were »» all gorge and famous in our last lives »» in the glories of the 80's you said »» 'the end is nothing to fear' I said »» - blow the end - nowbaby »» who do I gotta shag to get outta here »» and then when it all seemed clear »» just then you go and disappear

»»» sure you're out there orbiting around »»» wish I had you back now »»» I met a drag king call venus »»» she had a velvet hologram she said »»» 'my husband ran off with my »»» shaman but they love me as I am' »»» in the glories of the 80's »»» I may not have to die »»» I'll clone myself »»» like that blonde chick »»» that sings Bette Davis Eyes »»» and then when it all seemed clear »»» just then you go »»» and »»» disappear

Graveyard

here, I said
don't even let this go
and it's, hey, to that old man
I'm coming in the graveyard
with my little tune
it's june, I said
she's gone
but I'm alive, I'm alive
I'm coming in the graveyard
to sing you to sleep now

Happy phantom

and if I die today I'll be the HAPPY phantom and I'll go chasin' the nuns out in the yard and I'll run naked through the streets without my mask on and I will never need umbrellas in the rain I'll wake up in strawberry fields every day and the atrocities of school I can forgive the HAPPY phantom has no right to bitch *oo who the time is getting closer oo who time to be a ghost oo who every day we're getting closer the sun is getting dim will we pay for who we been* so if I die today I'll be the HAPPY phantom and I'll go wearin' my NAUGHTIES like a jewel they'll be my ticket to the universal opera there's Judy Garland taking Buddha by the hand and then these seven little men get up to dance they say Confucius does his crossword with a pen I'm still the angel to a girl who hates to SIN or will I see you dear and wish I could come back you found a girl that you could TRULY love again will you still call for me when she falls asleep or do we soon forget the things we cannot see

HEY JUPITER

no one's picking up the phone
guess it's me and me
and this little masochist
she's ready to confess
all the things that I never thought
that she could feel and

hey Jupiter
nothings been the same
so are you gay
are you blue
thought we both could use a friend
to run to
and I thought you'd see with me
you wouldn't have to be something new
sometimes I breathe you in

and I know you know
and sometimes you take a swim
found your writing on my wall
if my hearts soaking wet
Boy your boots can leave a mess
hey Jupiter
nothings been the same
so are you gay
are you blue
thought we both could use a friend
to run to
and I thought I wouldn't have to keep
with you
hiding

thought I knew myself so well
all the dolls I had
took my leather off the shelf
your apocalypse was fab
for a girl who couldn't choose between
the shower or the bath

and I thought I wouldn't have to be
with you
a magazine

no one's picking up the phone
guess it's clear he's gone

and this little masochist
is lifting up her dress
guess I thought I could never feel
the things I feel
hey Jupiter

Here. in my head

In my head I found you there
and running around and following me
but you don't dare
but I find that I have, now, more
than I ever wanted to

so maybe Thomas Jefferson wasn't born
in your backyard like you have said and
maybe I'm just the horizon you run to when she has left
you there you are, here in my head and
running around and calling me "come back
I'll show you the roses that brush off the snow and
open their petals again and again" and you know that
apple green ice cream can melt in your hands I can't so I

held your hand at the fair and
even forgot what time it was
and even Thomas Jefferson wasn't born
in your backyard like you have said and
maybe I'm just the horizon you run to
when she has left you and me here alone on the floor
you're counting my feathers as the bells toll
you see the bow and belt and the girl from the south all
favorites of mine you know them all well
and spring brings fresh little puddles that makes it all clear makes it all
do you know what this is doing to me
here in my head.

Home on the range: Cherokee Edition

Oh give me a home where the buffalo roam
where the deer and the antelope play
where seldom is heard a discouraging word
and the skies are not cloudy all day

home home on the range
where the deer and the antelope play
where seldom is heard a discouraging word
and the skies are not cloudy all day

well Jackson made deals, a thief down to his heels
hello trail of tears
the Smokies could hide a Cherokee bride,
her brave was shot yesterday.

home home on the range
where the deer and the antelope play
where seldom is heard a discouraging word
and the skies are not cloudy all day

we know it's not Caroline
your home is your home
the range may be fine for some but not in my eyes
home home on the range
the Smokies always hide a
Cherokee bride but in her eyes
We know it's not Caroline.

America
who discovered your ass
the white man came "this land is my land
this is your land" they sang

home home on the range
where the deer and the antelope play
where seldom is heard a discouraging word
and the skies are not cloudy all day

Horses

I got me some horses
to ride on
to ride on
they say that your demons
can't go there
so I got me some Horses
to ride on
to ride on
as long as your army
keeps perfectly still
and maybe I'll find me a sailor
a tailor
and maybe together
we'll make mother well
so I got me some Horses
to ride on
to ride on
as long as your army
keeps perfectly still
you showed me the meadow
and Milkwood
and Silkwood
and you would if I would
but you never would
so I chased down your posies
your pansies in my hosies
then opened my hands
and they were empty then

off with Superfly
counting your bees
oh me honey like
one two three
the camera is rolling
it's easy like
one
two
three
and if there is a way to find you
I will find you
but you will find me if Neil
makes me a tree an afro a pharaoh
I can't go
you said so
and threads that are golden
don't break easily

HONEY

A little dust never stopped me none he liked my shoes I kept them on
sometimes I can hold my tongue sometimes not,
when you just skip-to-loo my darlin'
and you know what you're doin' so don't even

you're just too used to my honey now
you're just too used to my honey

and I think I could leave your world
if she was the better girl
so when we died I tried to bribe the undertaker
cause I'm not sure what you're doin' or the reasons

you're just too used to my honey now
you're just too used to my honey

don't bother coming down
I made a friend of the western sky
don't bother coming down
you always liked your babies tight

turn back one last time love to watch those cowboys ride
but cowboys know cowgirls ride on the Indian side
and you know what you're doin' so don't even

you're just too used to my honey now
you're just too used to my honey

Hotel

Met'em in a Hotel . Met'em in a Hotel . Beneath ground. tell me that he's missing . tell me this is one for . Lollipop Gestapo You were wild . where are you now . you were wild . where are you now give me more . give me more . give me more I have to learn to let you crash down . I have to learn to let you crash down . I have to learn to let you crash Met'em in a Hotel . Met'em in a Hotel . you say he's the biggest thing . there'll be this year . I guess that what I'm seeking . I guess that what I'm seeking . isn't here Met him in a Hotel . Met him in a guess world . guessed anyone but you you were wild . where are you now . you were wild . where are you now give me more . give me more . give me more . I have to learn to let you crash down where are the velvets . where are the velvets . where are the velvets . when you're coming   down
H   o   t   e   l
you were wild . where are you now . you were wild . where are you now
King Solomon's Mines . Exit 75 . I'm still alive . I'm still alive . I'm still alive

Humpty Dumpty

Humpty Dumpty sat on the wall
Humpty Dumpty had a great, great fall and
all the king's horses and all the king's men
couldn't put Humpty together again

Humpty Dumpty and Betty Louise
stole a Sony and some Camembert cheese
and she said "Humpty baby
take me to the river
cause I like the way it runs
take me to the river
you know I like the way it runs"

he said "ah, ooh, everything's going my way"
he said "maybe it's my lucky day"
I said "anything you want I can give"
she said "I want to take your picture, mm, just for me"
he said "anything"
she said "up there baby get on the wall babe"

Humpty Dumpty sat on the wall
and looked at her as he was falling and
all the king's horses and all the king's men
couldn't put Humpty together again

hey Betty Louise Betty Louise
she said "I like custard in the summer, honey"
what it takes to be Queen
what it takes to be Queen
what it takes to be

Hungarian wedding song

when you said you'd marry me
I thought you meant you wanted to
then I thought you'd like to
maybe on a Tuesday

all the dead are coming
I heard they'll be dressing
something kind of maggoty
rolling with the froperty
may not want to include

ICICLE

Icicle Icicle where are you going I have a hiding place when spring marches in will you keep watch for me I hear them calling gonna lay down gonna lay down

greeting the monster in our Easter dresses Father says bow your head like the Good Book says well I think the Good Book is missing some pages gonna lay down gonna lay down

and when my hand touches myself I can finally rest my head and when they say 'take of his body' I think I'll take from mine instead

Getting Off Getting Off while they're all downstairs singing prayers sing away he's in my pumpkin p.j.'s lay your book on my chest feel the word feel the word feel the word feel it

I could have I should have I could have flown you know I could have I should have I didn't so

IIEEE

with your E's
and your ease
and I do one more
need a lip gloss boost
in your america
is it God's
is it yours
sweet saliva
with your E's
and your ease
and I do one more
I know we're dying
and there's no sign of a parachute
we scream in cathedrals
why can't it be beautiful
why does there
gotta be a sacrifice
just say yes
you little arsonist
you're so sure you can save
every hair on my chest
just say yes
you little arsonist
with your E's
and your ease
and I do one more
well I know we're dying
and there's no sign of a parachute
in this chapel
little chapel of love
can't we get a little grace
and some elegance
no we scream in cathedrals
why can't it be beautiful
why does there
gotta be a sacrifice

In the Springtime of his Voodoo

Standin on a corner in Winslow Arizona
and I'm quite sure I'm in the wrong song
2 girls 65 got a piece tied up in the
back seat
"honey we're Recovering Christians"

in the Springtime of his voodoo
he was going to show me spring

and right there for a minute
I knew you so well

got an angry snatch
girls you know what I mean
when swivelin that hip doesn't do the trick
me pureed sanitarily Mr Sulu
warp speed
warp speed
warp speed
in the Springtime of his voodoo

every road leads back to my door
every road I will follow
every road leads back to my door
got all your crosses loaded

and I know she's not that
Foxy
Boys
I said I know she's not that
Foxy but
you gotta owe something sometimes
you gotta owe boys
when you're your momma's sunshine
you've got to give something sometimes
when you're the sweetest cherry
in an apple pie
I need some voodoo on these prunes
in the Springtime of his voodoo
he was going to show me spring

JACKIE'S STRENGTH

a Bouvier till her wedding day shots rang out the police came.mama laid me on the front lawn and prayed for Jackie's strength . feeling old by 21 . never thought my day would come . my bridesmaids getting laid I pray for Jackie's strength . make me laugh . say you know what you want . you said we were the real thing . so I show you some more and I learn . what black magic can do . make me laugh . say you know you can turn . me into the real thing . so I show you some more . and I learn . stickers licked on lunch boxes worshipping David Cassidy . yeah I mooned him once on Donna's box . she's still in recovery . sleep-overs Beene's got some pot . you're only popular with anorexia so I turn myself inside out . in hope someone will see . make me laugh . say you know what you want you said we were the real thing . so I show you some more and I learn . what black magic can do . make me laugh . say you know you can turn . me into the real thing so I show you some more . and I learn . I got lost on my wedding day typical the police came . but virgins always get backstage no matter what they've got to say . if you love enough you'll lie a lot . guess they did in camelot . mama's waiting on my front lawn . I pray I pray I pray . for Jackie's strength

JOSEPHINE

not tonight Josephine,

in an army's strength therein
lies the denouement. From
here you're haunting me. By
the Seine so beautiful, only
not to be of use — impossible.

so strange, victory — 1,200
spires, the only sound,
Moscow burning. Empty like
the Tuileries. Like a dream
Vienna seems, only not to
be of use — impossible.

In the last extremity — to
advance or not to advance —
I hear you laughing.

even still you're calling me
"not tonight, not tonight,

not tonight"

Josephine

JUST ELLEN

ever since I met you, you captured my heart
you treated me like a lady from the very start
guess I'm a little girl in her dreams
who doesn't want to see
that I have to grow older and change on my own
I want to be a singer, but go it alone
but it is so hard for me cause I don't want to see that

I'm too young for a man
but I'm too old for a boy
so can't we just pretend
that I am older than I really am
but then, only little girls pretend

I put on all the make-up that I can possibly find
I'm five years older in just a minute's time
but I can't compete with the ladies that attract your kind
so I rummage through my sister's things
hoping to find something that will catch your eye
to make you change your mind
so I won't have to leave, so you won't say to me

I'm too young for a man
but I'm too old for a boy
so can't we just pretend
that I am older than I really am
but then, only little girls pretend

I'm left out in the night
I've lost all my senses
I know this isn't right
but you've captured my defenses
I really am in love
well that's the way I feel
this game has to stop
cause you know it can't be real

I'm too young for a man
but I'm too old for a boy
so can't we just pretend
that I am older than I really am
but then, only little girls pretend

I know I'd make you happy
but I'm too young for a wife
love is always special but I know I can't rush life
so I'm waiting in the wings to see what life will bring
and maybe in a few years when I am wise and tall
love will light again and shine upon us all
he says I'm a little girl in her dreams
who doesn't want to see

I'm too young for a man
but I'm too old for a boy
so can't we just pretend
that I am older than I really am
but then, only little girls pretend

JUÁREZ

dropped off the edge again
down in Juárez »»» "don't even
bat an eye »»» if the eagle
cries" the rasta man says, just
cause the desert likes »»»
young girls flesh and »»» no
angel came.

I don't think you even know
»»» what you think you just
said »»» so go on spill your
seed »»» shake your gun to
the rasta man's head »»» and
the desert - she must be
blessed and »»» no angel
came.

there's a time to keep it up »»»
a time to keep it in »»» the
Indian is told »»» the cowboy
is his friend »»» you know that
I can breathe »»» even when I
cheat »»» should. should've
been over for me »»» no angel
came.

LEATHER

look I'm standing naked
before you don't you want more than
my sex I can scream as loud as your
last one but I can't claim innocence
oh god could it be the weather *oh god
why am I here if love isn't forever and
it's NOT THE WEATHER hand me
my leather* I could just pretend that
you love me the night would lose all
sense of fear but why do I need you
to love me when you can't hold what
I hold dear I almost ran over an
angel he had a nice big fat cigar "IN
A SENSE" he said "you're alone here
so if you jump you best jump far"

LIQUID DIAMONDS

surrender then start your engines
you'll know quite soon what my mistake
was
for those on horseback or dog sled
you turn on at the bend in the road
I hear she stills grants forgiveness
although I willingly forgot her
the offering is molasses and you say
I guess I'm an underwater thing so I
guess I can't take it personally
I guess I'm an underwater thing I'm
liquid running
there's a sea secret in me
it's plain to see it is rising
but I must be flowing liquid diamonds
calling for my soul
at the corners of the world
I know she's playing poker with the rest of the stragglers calling for my soul at the
corners of the world I know she's playing poker and if your friends don't come back
to you and you know this is madness a lilac mess in your prom dress and you say I
guess I'm an underwater thing

LITTLE AMSTERDAM

Little Amsterdam
In a southern town
hominy get it on the plate girl
Momma keep your head down
Momma it wasn't my bullet

don't take me back to the Range
I'm just comin out of the cell in my brain
cause girl you got to know these days
which side your on

Momma got shit
she loved a brown man
then she built a bridge in the Sheriff's bed
she'd do anything to save her man
you see her olives are cold pressed
and her best friend is a sun dress
but Momma
it wasn't my bullet

round and a round and a round I go
round and a round this time for keeps
Father only you can save my soul
and playing that organ must count
for something
girl you got to know these days
which side your on
Little Amsterdam
shut down today
they buried her with a
butter bean bouquet
and the Sheriff now can't ride away
like he said into the sunset
and I won't say
he shouldna paid
but Momma
it wasn't my bullet

LITTLE EARTHQUAKES

yellow bird
flying get shot in the wing good year for
hunters and Christmas parties and I
hate and I hate and I hate and I hate
elevator music the way we fight the
way I'm left here silent oh these little
earthquakes here we go again these little earthquakes doesn't take much to
RIP us into pieces we danced in grave-
yards with vampires till dawn we
laughed in the faces of kings never
afraid to burn and I hate and I hate
and I hate and I hate disintegration
watching us wither black winged roses
that safely changed their COLOR I
can't reach you I can't reach you give
me life give me pain give me myself again

Lust

hey you gender nectar sifting through the grain of gold »»» tripping at your door is that you. alpha in her blood »»» and when the woman lies you don't believe her »»» rolling and unrolling coiling emerging running free »»» running through the underworld into your room

is he real or a ghost-lie she feels she isn't heard »»» and the veil tears and rages till her voices are »»» remembered and his secrets can be told

hey you gender nectar crystalline from the vine »»» you know you'll drink her rolling and unrolling »»» coiling emerging running free running through »»» the afterworld into your room so she prays »»» for a prankster and lust in the marriage bed »»» and he waits till she can give and he »»» waits and he waits

MARIANNE

tuna
rubber
a little blubber in my igloo
and I knew you pigtails and all
girls when they fall
and they said Marianne killed herself
and I said not a chance
don't you love the girls ladies babes
old bags who say she was so pretty why
why why why did she crawl down in the old
deep ravine

c'mon pigtails girls and all those sailors
get your bags and hold down won't you just
hold down cause Ed is watching my every sound
I said
they're watching my every sound

the weasel squeaks faster than a seven day week
I said Timmy and that purple Monkey
are all down
at Bobby's house
making themselves pesters and lesters and jesters and my
traitors of kind
and I'm just having thoughts of Marianne
she could outrun the fastest slug
she could
Marianne
quickest girl in the frying pan

Mary

Everybody wants something from you
everybody want a piece of Mary
lush valley all dressed in green
just ripe for the picking

god I want to get you out of here
you can ride in a pink Mustang
when I think of what we've done to you
Mary can you hear me

growing up isn't always fun
they tore your dress and stole your ribbons
they see you cry they lick their lips
well butterflies don't belong in nets

Mary can you hear me
Mary you're bleeding, Mary don't be afraid
we're just waking up and I hear help is on the way
Mary can you hear me
Mary, like Jimmy said, Mary don't be afraid
"cause even the wind even the wind cries your name"

everybody wants you sweetheart
everybody got a dream of glory
Las Vegas got a pinup girl
they got her armed as they buy and sell her
rivers of milk running dry
can't you hear the dolphins crying
what'll we do when our babies scream
fill their mouths with some acid rain

Mary can you hear me
Mary you're bleeding, Mary don't be afraid
we're just waking up and I hear help is on the way
Mary can you hear me
Mary, like Jimmy said, Mary don't be afraid
"cause even the wind even the wind cries your name"

Me and a gun

5am friday morning thursday night far from sleep I'm still up and driving can't go home obviously so I'll just change direction cause they'll soon know where I live and I wanna live got a full tank and some chips it was me and a gun and man on my back and I sang "holy holy" as he buttoned down his pants me and a gun and a man on my back but I haven't seen BARBADOS so I must get out of this yes I wore a slinky red thing does that mean I should spread for you, your friends your father, Mr. Ed and I know what this means me and Jesus a few years back used to hand and he said "it's your choice babe just remember I don't think you'll be back in 3 days time so you choose well" tell me what's right is it my right to be on my stomach of Fred's Seville and do you know CAROLINA where the biscuits are soft and sweet these things go through your head when there's a man on your back and you're pushed flat on your stomach it's not a classic cadillac

Merman

go to bed
the priests are dead
now no one
can call you bad
go to bed
the priests are dead
finally you're in peppermint land

he's a merman
he doesn't need your voice
he's a merman

go to bed
dream instead
and you will find him
he's a merman
to the knee
doesn't need something you're not willing to give
he's a merman
doesn't need your voice to cross his lands of ice

go to bed
the priests are dead
now no one
can call you bad
go to bed
the priests are dead
finally you found him

let it out
who could ever say you're not simply wonderful
who could ever harm you
sleep now
you're my little goat

go to bed
the priests are dead
and come sing it all again
go to bed
past the apple orchard
and you'll feel nice

two can play
I said, two can play

MOTHER

go go go go now out of the nest it's
time to go go go now circus girl without a safety
net here here now don't cry you raised your hand
for the assignment tuck those ribbons under your
helmet be a good soldier first my left foot then
my right behind the OTHER pantyhose running
in the cold *mother the car is here somebody leave*
the light on green limousine for the redhead
DANCING dancing girl and when I dance for him
somebody leave the light on just in case I like the
dancing I can remember where I come from I
walked into your dream and now I've forgotten
how to dream my own dream you are the
CLEVER one aren't you brides in veils for you we
told you all of our secrets all but one so don't you
even try the phone has been disconnected drip-
ping with blood and with time and with your
advice poison me against the MOON I escape into
your escape into our very favorite fearscape it's
across the sky and I cross my heart and I cross my
legs oh my god first my left foot then my right
behind the other breadcrumbs lost under the snow

Mr Zebra

hello Mr Zebra
can I have your sweater
cause it's cold cold cold
in my hole hole hole
Ratatouille Strychnine
sometimes she's a friend of mine

with a gigantic whirlpool
that will blow your mind

hello Mr Zebra
ran into some confusion with a Mrs Crocodile
furry mussels marching on
she thinks she's Kaiser Wilhelm
or a civilized syllabub
to blow your mind
figure it out
she's a goodtime fella
she got a little fund to fight for Moneypenny's rights
figure it out
she's a goodtime fella
too bad the burial was premature she said
and smiled

MUHAMMAD MY FRIEND

Muhammad my friend
it's time to tell the world
we both know it was a girl back in Bethlehem
and on that fateful day
when she was crucified
she wore Shiseido Red and we drank tea
by her side

sweet sweet
used to be so sweet to me

Muhammad my friend
I'm getting very scared
teach me how to love my brothers
who don't know the law
and what about the deal on the flying
trapeze got a peanut butter hand
but honey do drop in at the
Dew Drop Inn

sweet sweet
between the boys and the bees
and Moses I know
I know you've seen fire
but you've never seen fire
until you've seen Pele blow
and I've never seen light
but I sure have seen gold
and Gladys save a place for me
on your grapevine
till I get my own TV show

ashre ashre ashre ashre
and if I lose my Cracker Jacks at the
tidal wave I got a place
in the Pope's rubber robe
Muhammad my friend
it's time to tell the world
we both know it was a girl
back in Bethlehem

Never seen blue

some boy you are
to take me by the hand
through an elevator
got a little red line
that tells you, boy,
where the razor's been

you said, girl if you think
you can turn that violator
you'll finally be that woman
finally be that woman
that's been frozen
in that pretty silver gown

I've never seen blue
like the blues he drives
in and around
and through me again
I said, I've never seen eyes
like the blues he drives
in and around
and through me again
through me again
through me again

some boy you are
to wear my color red
to wear it very proudly
wear it like a lady
knows how to cross her legs
where the birdie's been

I've never seen blue
like the blues he drives
in and around
and through me again
said I've never seen eyes
like the blues he drives
in and around
and through me again
through me again
through me again

Not the Red Baron

Not the Red Baron
Not Charlie Brown
think I got the message figured
another pilot down
and are their devils with halos
in beautiful capes
taking them into the flames

Not Judy G
Not Jean Jean
with a hallowed
heart
I see that screen go
down in the flames
with every step with
every beautiful heel
pointed

Not the Red Baron I'm sure
Not Charlie's wonderful dog
not anyone I really know
just another pilot down
maybe I'll just sing him a last
little sound many there
know some girls
with red ribbons
the prettiest
red
ribbons

1000 Oceans

these tears I've cried. I've cried 1000 oceans »»» and if it seems I'm. floating. in the darkness »»» well, I can't believe that I would keep. keep you from flying. »»» and I would cry 1000 more if that's what it takes »»» to sail you home »»» sail you home. sail you home.

I'm aware what the rules are. but you know that I »»» will run. you know that I will follow you. »»» over silbury hill through the solar field. you know that I will follow you

and if I find you. will you. still remember »»» playing at trains. or does this little blue ball »»» just fade away. over silbury hill through the solar field. »»» you know that I will follow you. »»» I'm aware what the rules are but you know that I »»» will run. you know that I will follow you.

these tears I've cried. I've cried. 1000 oceans »»» and if it seems I'm. floating. in the darkness »»» well, I can't believe that I would keep.

keep you from flying. »»» so I will cry 1000 more if that's what it takes »»» to sail you home. »»» sail you home. sail. sail you home.

Northern Lad

Had a northern lad
well not exactly had
he moved like the sunset
god who painted that
first he loved my accent
how his knees could bend
I thought we'd be ok
me and my molasses
But I feel something is wrong
But I feel this cake just isn't done
Don't say that you Don't
and if you could see me now
said if you could see me now
girls you've got to know
when it's time to turn the page
when you're only wet
because of the rain
he don't show much these days
it gets so fucking cold
I loved his secret places
but I can't go anymore
"you change like sugar cane"
says my northern lad
I guess you go too far
when pianos try to be guitars
I feel the west in you
and I feel it falling apart too
Don't say that you Don't
and if you could see me now
said if you could see me now
girls you've got to know
when it's time to turn the page
when you're only wet
because of the rain
when you're only wet
because of the rain

Ode to the Banana King (Part 1)

Turning back ten thousand years
it's all a blur where the taxis go
monster man a willing friend
lucy serves the melon cold

violent and delicious souls
four red trucks dressed illegally
mother knows how the bugle blows
gonna get caught gonna get caught
gonna get caught in her rug

this is not a conclusion
no revolution
just a little confusion
on where your head has been

boats made out of paper float
dreams made up for the Banana King. darling
crumbs you have lapped freely of
devious we all have been

violent and delicious souls
violent and delicious souls
this is not a conclusion
no revolution
just a little confusion
on where your head has been

PANDORA'S AQUARIUM

Pandora
Pandora's aquarium
she dives for shells
with her nautical nuns
and thoughts you thought
you'd never tell I am not asking you to believe in me Boy I think you're confused
I'm not Persephone foam can be dangerous with tape across my mouth these
things you do I never asked you how Line me up in single file with all your
grievances Stare but I can taste you're still alive below the waste ripples come and
ripples go
and ripple back to me Pandora Pandora's aquarium

she dives for shells
with her nautical nuns
and thoughts you thought
you'd never tell
Line me up in single file
with all your grievances
Stare but I can taste
you're still alive below the waste
ripples come and ripples
go and ripple back to me
I am not asking you to believe in
me Boy I think you're confused
I'm not Persephone
She's in New York somewhere
checking her accounts
The Lord of the Flies was
diagnosed as Sound

PAST THE MISSION

I don't believe I went too far I said I was willing she said she knew what my books did not I thought she knew what's up

Past the mission behind the prison tower past the mission I once knew a hot girl past the mission they're closing every hour past the mission I smell the roses

She said they all think they know him well she knew him better everyone wanted something from him I did too but I shut my mouth he just gave me a smile

Hey they found a body not sure it was his but they're using his name and she gave him shelter and somewhere I know she knows somethings only she knows

PLAYBOY MOMMY

In my platforms . I hit the floor . fell face down . didn't help my brain out . then the baby came . before I found . the magic how . to keep her happy . I never was the fantasy . of what you want . wanted me to be . Don't judge me so harsh little girl . so . you got a playboy mommy . but when you tell em my name . and you want to cross that . Bridge all on your own . little girl they'll do you no harm . cause they know. Your playboy mommy . but when you tell em my name . from here to Birmingham I got a few friends . I never was there was there when it counts . I get my way . you're so like me . you seemed ashamed. ashamed that I was . a good friend of American soldiers . I'll say it loud here by your grave . those angels can't . ever take my place . somewhere where the orchids grow . I can't find those church bells . that played when you died . played Gloria . talkin bout . Hosanah . don't judge me so harsh little girl .

THE POOL

one
with her hands open
don't be afraid, she said
no one will know it
just you and me
and when it's over
I'll go back

PRETTY GOOD YEAR

Tears on the sleeve of a man don't wanna be a boy today heard the eternal footman
bought himself a bike to race and Greg he writes letters and burns his CDs they
say you were something in those formative years hold on to nothing as fast as you
can well still pretty good year

Maybe a bright sandy beach is gonna bring you back may not so now you're off
you're gonna see America well let me tell you something about America pretty
good year some things are melting now well what's it gonna take till my baby's
alright

and Greg he writes letters with his birthday pen sometimes he's aware that
they're drawing him in Lucy was pretty your best friend agreed well still pretty
good year

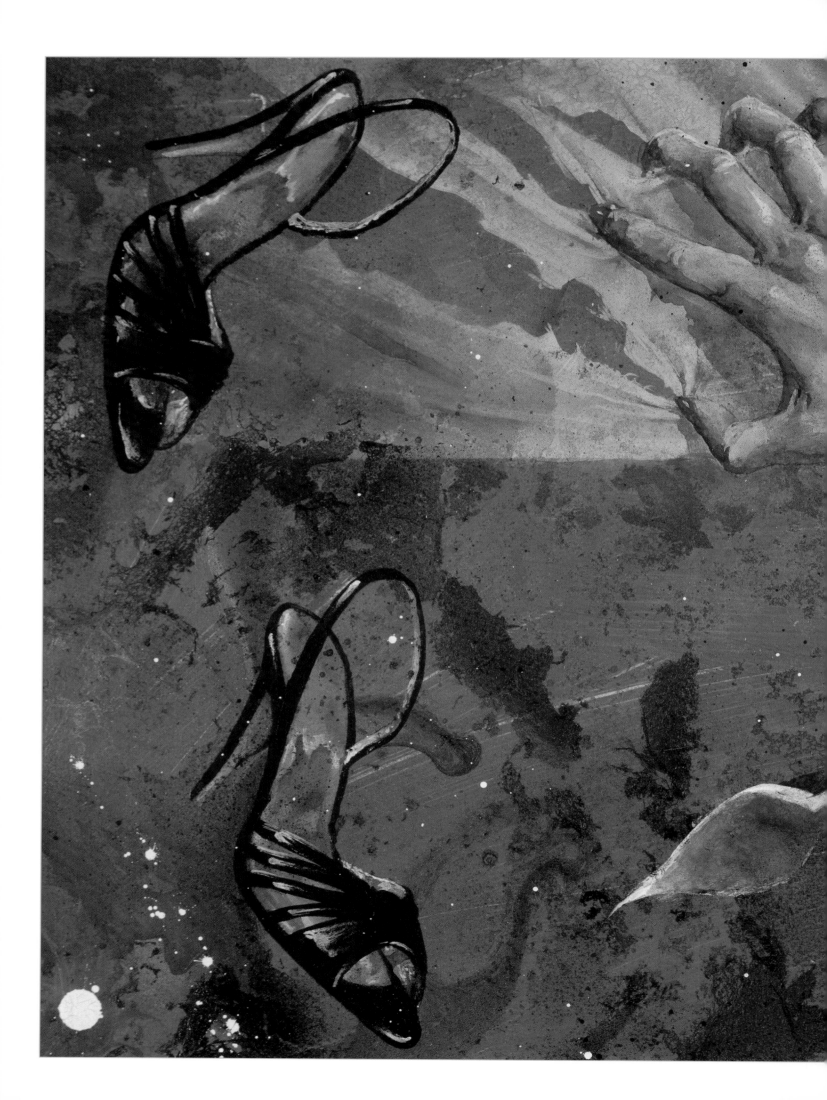

PRECIOUS THINGS

so I ran faster but it caught me here yes my loyalties turned like my ankle in the seventh grade running after BILLY running after the rain *these precious things let them bleed let them wash away these precious things let them break their hold over me* he said you're really an ugly girl but I like the way you play and I died but I thanked him can you believe that sick holding on to his picture dressing up every day I wanna smash the faces of those beautiful BOYS those christian boys so you can make me cum that doesn't make you Jesus I remember yes in my peach party dress no one dared no one cared to tell me where the pretty girls are those demigods with their NINE-INCH nails and little fascist panties tucked inside the heart of every nice girl

PROFESSIONAL WIDOW

slag pit
stag shit
honey bring it close to my lips
yes
don't blow those brains yet
we gotta be big boy
we gotta be big
starfucker just like my Daddy
just like my Daddy selling his baby
just like my Daddy

gonna strike a deal make him feel
like a Congressman
it runs in the family
gonna strike a deal make him feel
like a Congressman
it runs in the family

rest your shoulders Peaches and Cream
everywhere a Judas as far as you can see
beautiful angel
calling "we got every re-run of Muhammad Ali"

prism perfect
honey bring it close to your lips
yes
what is termed a landslide of principle
proportion boy it gotta be big boy
starfucker just like my Daddy
just like my Daddy selling his baby
just like my Daddy
gonna strike a deal make him feel
like a Congressman
it runs in the family
Mother Mary
china white
brown may be sweeter

she will supply
Mother Mary
china white
brown may be sweeter
she will supply
she will supply
she will supply
she will supply

Purple People

well hey do you do judo when they surround you
a little mental Yoga will they disappear
it's grim but never dubious as motives go
one thing she always promise, promise is a show
thunder wishes it could be the snow
wishes it could be as loved as she can be
these gifts are here for her, for you, for me

I watch me be this other thing I never know
if I'm marooned or where the purple people go
then lily white matricide from vicious words
it doesn't leave a scratch so therefore no one's hurt
thunder wishes it could be the snow
wishes it could be as loved as she can be
these gifts are here for her, for you, for me

and on and on the nurses make it clear
just when you escape you have yourself to fear
a restaurant that never has to close
breakfast every hour it could save the world

so hey do you do judo in your finery
an angel's face is tricky to wear constantly
thunder wishes it could be the snow
wishes it could be as loved as she can be
these gifts are here for her, for you, for me
for her for her

Raspberry Swirl

I am not your señorita
I am not from your tribe
in the garden I did no crime
I am not your señorita
I am not from your tribe
if you want inside her
well,
boy you better make her raspberry swirl
things are getting desperate
when all the boys can't be men
everybody knows
I'm her friend
everybody knows
I'm her man
I am not your señorita
I don't aim so high
in my heart I did no crime
if you want inside her
well,
boy you better make her raspberry swirl

Putting The Damage On

glue
stuck to my shoes
does anyone know why you play with
an orange rind
you say you packed my things
and divided what was mine you're off to
the mountain top
I say her skinny legs could use sun
but now I'm wishing
for my best impression
of my best Angie Dickinson
but now I've got to worry
cause boy you still look pretty
when you're putting the damage on

don't make me scratch on your door
I never left you
for a Banjo

I only just turned around for a poodle
and a corvette
and my impression
of my best Angie Dickinson
but now I've got to worry
cause boy you still look pretty
when you're putting the damage on

I'm trying not to move
it's just your ghost
passing through
I said
I'm trying not to move
it's just your ghost passing through
it's just your ghost
passing through
and now
I'm quite sure
there's a light in your platoon
I never seen a light move
like yours
can do to me
so now I'm wishing
for my best impression
of my best Angie Dickinson
but now I've got to worry
cause boy you still look pretty
to me
but I've got a place to go
I've got a ticket to your late show
and now I'm worrying cause even still
you sure are pretty
when you're putting the damage on
yes
when you're putting the damage on
you're just so pretty
when you're putting the damage on

Riot Poof

you know what you know so
you go break the terror of the
urban spell »»» this alliance
you say 'I'm on the threshold
of greatness girl' »»» so you
burn your pagoda through the
congo till there's a broken
bond »»» on the birth of the
search white trash my native
son

it will all find its way in time

blossom, riot poof

you know what you know so
you go chain her to your flow
»»» she bites through your
dried lean meat as she's
going to the movie show »»»
in a bath of glitter and a tiny
shiver she crawls through
your java sea »»» black
sahara I'm stepping in to your
space oddity

it will all find its way in time

blossom, riot poof

the sun is warming my man is
moistening »»» on the bomb
on the bond on the bomb

RUBIES AND GOLD

Rubies and Gold
star of my moonlight
warmer than roses in spring
The kingdoms were sold
to hold their beauty, well
I'd sell my life anyway
just to say I held their heart in my arms
there's strength in my soul

Rubies and Gold
are you to me
You're a jewel upon my chest
warming my heart with your kisses,
a peaceful way to rest
fulfilling my life long wishes

And silently you're watching me
stroking my cheek with your hand
your eyes are deep yet filled with tears
I've never seen so much love in a man.

Rubies and Gold
star of my moonlight
warmer than roses in spring
The kingdoms were sold
to hold their beauty, well
I'd sell my life anyway
just to say I held their heart in my arms
there's strength in my soul

Rubies and Gold
you are to me

SHE'S YOUR COCAINE

She's your Cocaine
She's got you shaving your legs
you can suck anything
but you know you wanna be me
put on your make-up boy
you're your favourite stranger
and we all like to watch
So shimmy once and do it again
Bring your sister if you can't handle it
she says control it
then she says don't control it
then she says you're controlling
the way she makes you crawl
She's your Cocaine your Exodus laughing
and she knows what you are
so shimmy once and do it again
Bring your sister
Bring your sister if you can't handle it
If you want me to
Boy I could lie to you
you don't need one of these to let me inside of you
and is it true that devils end up like you
something safe for the picture frame
and is it true that devils end up like you
So tied up you don't know how she came
She's your Cocaine
She's got you shaving your legs
she got you liking mine back
got me taking it in
getting mine back
lasting mine evil
I'm taking my easel
and I'm writing good checks
you sign Prince of Darkness
try squire of dimness
please don't help me with this

Siren

and you know you're
gonna lie to you
in your own way

know know too well
know the chill
know she breaks
my Siren

NEVER was one
for a
prissy girl
coquette
Call in For
an ambulance
Reach high
doesn't
mean SHE'S
holy
just means
She's got a Cellular
handy
almost
Brave
almost
pregnant
almost in love "VANILLA"

and you know you're
gonna lie to you
in your own way

SILENT ALL THESE YEARS

excuse me but can I be you for a while my DOG won't bite if you sit real still I got the anti-Christ in the kitchen yellin' at me again yeah I can hear that been saved again by the garbage truck I got something to say you know but NOTHING comes yes I know what you think of me you never shut-up yeah I can hear that *but what if I'm a mermaid in these jeans of his with her name still on it hey but I don't care cause sometimes I said sometimes I hear my voice and its been HERE silent all these years* so you found a girl who thinks really deep thoughts what's so amazing about really deep thoughts boy you best pray that I bleed real soon how's that thought for you my scream got lost in a paper cup you think there's a heaven where some screams have gone I got 25 bucks and a cracker do you think it's enough to get us there years go by will I still be waiting for somebody else to understand years go by if I'm stripped of my beauty and the orange clouds raining in my head years go by will I choke on my tears till finally there is nothing left one more casualty you know we're too EASY easy easy well I love the way we communicate your eyes focus on my funny lip shape let's hear what you think of me now but baby don't look up in the sky is falling your MOTHER shows up in a nasty dress it's your turn now to stand where I stand everybody lookin' at you here take hold of my hand yeah I can hear them

Sister Janet

Master Shaman, I have come with my dolly from the shadow side
with a demon and an Englishman. I'm my mother I'm my son
nobody else is slipping the blade in easy
nobody else is slipping the blade in the marmalade

but all the angels and all the wizards, black and white,
are lighting candles in our hands
can you feel them, yes, touching hands before our eyes
and I can even see sweet Marianne

Sister Janet, you have come from the woman clothed with the sun
your veil is quietly becoming none. Call the Wanderer he has gone
and all those up there are making it look so easy
with your perfect wings
a wing can cover all sorts of things

this again
well I think I could try this once again

and all the angels and all the wizards, black and white,
are lighting candles in our hands
can you feel them, yes, touching hands before our eyes
and I can even see sweet Marianne

Sister named Desire

got a sister named Desire
they don't let you light those little
boys by their house
on the backhand swing
I know a vicar who coughs a lot
thought we told some little
sweet stories in the parking lot

they say the girl lost her sway
they say the girl lost her sway that day

god I'd like to drag him for a long way
'cause maybe I...
then I'd just cry a little
tear near to that sleepy safe place
and I'm gonna take him by myself if I've got to go
don't let you, let you know where she goes to
with those, me as I interfere

the girl lost her sway
they say the girl lost her sway that day

teach me about them old worlds big brother man
in an elevator where
somebody can get out with the sound

they say that girl lost her sway
just watch it
just watch it slip through my hands, boy
watch it go
what you know

I. Yes.
I see, just see
'cause she still can swing

Song for Eric

I wait all day for my sailor and sometimes he comes
see you over hill and dale
riding on the wind I see
you know me you know me like the nightingale
"oh fair maiden, I see you standing there."
will you hold me for just a fair time
the tune is playing in the fair night
I see you in my dreams
fair boy your eyes haunt me

Spacedog

Way to go Mr. Microphone show us all what you don't know centuries secret societies he's our commander still space dog

so sure we were on something your feet are finally on the ground he said so sure we were on something your feet are just on the ground girl

rain and snow our engines have been receiving your eager call there's Colonel Dirtyfishydishcloth he'll distract her good don't worry so

and to the one you thought was on your side she can't understand she truly believes the lie

Lemon Pie he's coming through our commander still Space dog lines secure Space dog

Deck the halls I'm young again I'm you again racing turtles the grapefruit is winning seems I keep getting this story twisted so where's Neil when you need him deck the halls it's you again it's you again somewhere someone must know the ending is she still pissing in the river now heard she'd gone moved into a trailer park

so sure those girls now are in the Navy those bombs our friends can't even hurt you now and hold those tears cause they're still on your side don't hear the dogs barking don't say you know we've gone Andromeda stood with those girls before the hair in pairs it just got nasty and now those girls are gone

Spark

she's addicted to nicotine patches . she's addicted to nicotine patches
she's afraid of the light in the dark . 6.58 are you sure where my spark is
                                                                here
                                                                here . here
she's convinced she could hold back a glacier . but she couldn't keep Baby alive
doubting if there's a woman in there somewhere   here
you say you don't want it again . and again but you don't really mean it
you say you don't want it . this circus we're in
but you don't you don't really mean it you don't really mean it
if the Divine master plan is perfection . maybe next time I'll give Judas a try
trusting my soul to the ice cream assassin   here
you say you don't want it again . and again but you don't really mean it
you say you don't want it . this circus we're in
but you don't you don't really mean it you don't really mean it
how many fates turn around in the overtime
ballerinas that have fins that you'll never find
you thought that you were the bomb yeah well so did I
say you don't want it . say you don't want it . say you don't want it again
and again but you don't really mean it
say you don't want it . this circus we're in
but you don't you don't really mean it you don't really mean it
she's addicted to nicotine patches
she's afraid of the light in the dark
6.58 are you sure where my spark is   here

Spring Haze

well I know it's just a spring
haze »»» but I don't much like
the look of it »»» and if omens
are a god send like men »»»
breezing in »»» certain these
clouds go somewhere »»»
billowing out to somewhere
»»» in a single engine cessna
»»» you say we'll never make
it there »»» so all we do is
circle it

uh oh. let go. off on my way
»»» unseen this eternal
wanting »»» let go. way to go
so I get creamed »»» waiting
on Sunday to drown »»»
waiting on sunday to drown

and I know it's just a spring
haze »»» but I don't much like
the look of it »»» but all we do
is circle it »»» and I found out
where my edge is »»» and it
bleeds into where you resist
»»» and my only way out is to
go »»» so far in »»» billowing
out to somewhere »»»
billowing out luna riviera »»»
waiting on Sunday to land »»»
waiting on Sunday to drown
»»» why. does. it. always end
up like this »»» waiting on
Sunday so I get creamed »»»
waiting for Sunday to drown

SUGAR

Don't say morning's come
don't say it's up to me
if I could take twenty five minutes
out of the record books
sugar he brings me sugar

Bobby's collecting bees
and hammers he used one on me
cold war with little boys
get in with a bubble gum trade

sugar bring me sugar
I know the robins bring, bring me many things but
sugar he brings me sugar
as far as I can tell
I've been gone for miles now

and you know and I know I don't know me very well
and I know and you know if they found me out
sugar he brings me sugar
I know the robins bring they bring many things
sugar he brings me sugar

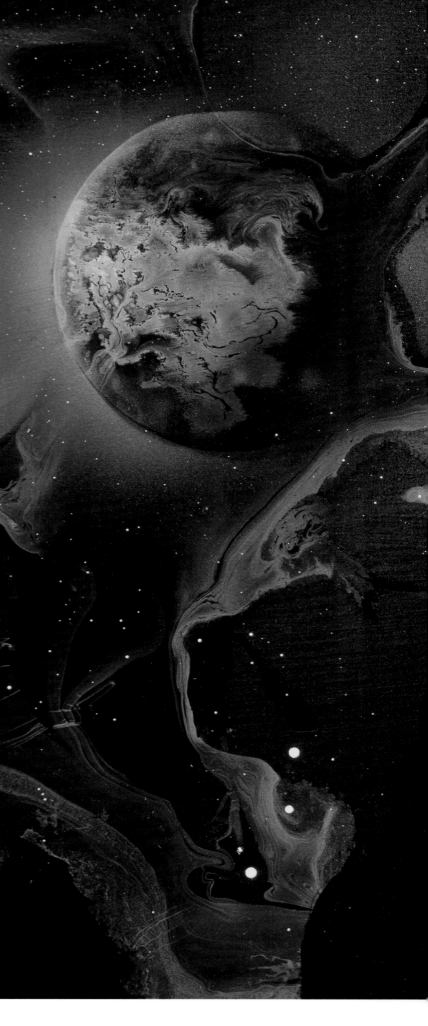

SUEDE

suede. you always felt like
suede. there are days I feel
your twin. »»» peekaboo.
hiding underneath your skin.
jets. are revving yes revving
»»» from a central source and
this. has power over me. not
because you feel »»»
something or don't feel
something for. me but be-
cause. mass. so big. it can
swallow swallow her whole
star intact. call me 'evil' call
me 'tide is on »»» your side'
anything that you want.
anybody knows you can
conjure »»» anything by the
dark of the moon. boy. and if
you keep your silence »»»
silencer on you'll talk yourself
right into a job. out of a hole.
into my »»» bayou. i'm sure
you've been briefed my
absorption lines. they are
frayed »»» and I fear. my fear
is greater than my faith but I
walk. the missionary way. »»»
you always felt like suede.
there are days I am your twin.
peekaboo. »»» hiding
underneath your skin. jets. are
revving yes revving from an
ether »»» twist. call me 'evil'.
little sister. I guess i'd do the
same. little sister. you'll
forgive me one day.

SWEET DREAMS

"Lie, lie, lies ev'rywhere," said the father to the son
your peppermint breath gonna choke 'em to death
daddy watch your little black sheep run
he got a knives in his back every time he opens up
you say, "he gotta be strong if he wanna be a man"
mister I don't know how you can have

sweet dreams sweet dreams.

land, land of liberty
we're run by a constipated man
when you live in the past
you refuse to see when your
daughter come home nine months pregnant
with five billion points of light
gonna shine em on the face of your friends
they got the earth in a sling
they got the world on her knees
they even got your zipper between their teeth

sweet dreams sweet dreams.

you say you say you say you have em I say that you're a liar
sweet dreams sweet dreams

go on, go on, go on and dream
your house is on fire
come along now

well, well, summer wind been catching up with me
"elephant mind, missy you don't have
you forgettin' to fly,
darlin', when you sleep"
I got a hazy lazy Susan
takin turns all over my dreams
I got lizards and snakes runnin' through my body
funny how they all have my face.

sweet dreams sweet dreams

TAKE TO THE SKY

This house is like Russia with eyes cold and grey
you got me moving in a circle, I dyed my hair red today

I just want a little passion to hold me in the dark
I know I got some magic buried, buried deep in my heart
but my priest says you ain't saving no souls
my father says you ain't makin' any money
my doctor says you just took it to the limit
and here I stand with this sword in my hand

you can say it one more time what you don't like
let me hear it one more time
then have a seat while I take to the sky

my heart is like the ocean it gets in the way
so close to touching freedom then I hear the guards call my name
and my priest says you ain't saving no souls
my father says you ain't makin' any money
my doctor says you just took it to the limit
and here I stand with this sword in my hand

you can say it one more time what you don't like
let me hear it one more time
then have a seat while I take to the sky

if you don't like me just a little, well, why do you hang around
if you don't like me just a little why do you take it

this house is like Russia
you can say it one more time you can say it one more time
you can say it one more time what you don't like
let me hear it one more time
then have a seat while I take to the sky

TALULA

Congratulate you
said you had a double tongue
balancing cake and bread
say goodbye to a glitter girl

Talula
Talula
you don't want to lose her
she must be worth losing
if it is worth something
Talula
Talula
she's brand new now to you
wrapped in your papoose
your little Fig Newton

say goodbye to the old world

ran into the Henchman who severed
Anne Boleyn
he did it right quickly a merciful man
she said 1 + 1 is 2
but Henry said that it was 3
so it was
here I am

Talula
Talula
I don't want to lose it
it must be worth something
Talula
Talula
she's brand new now to you
wrapped in your papoose
your little Fig Newton

and Jamaica
do you know what I have done
Mary M weaving on said
what you want is in the blood Senators
I got Big Bird on the fishing line
with a bit of a shout a bit of a shout
a bit of an angry snout
he's my favourite hooker of the whole bunch
and I know about his only Bride
and how the Russians die on the ice
I got my rape hat on
honey but I always could accessorise
and I never cared too much for the money
but I know right now
that it's in God's hands
oh but I don't know who the Father is

Talula
Talula
I don't want to lose him
he must be worth losing
if it is worth something
Talula
Talula
he's brand new now to you
wrapped in your papoose
your little Fig Newton

TEAR IN YOUR HAND

all the world just stopped now so you say you don't wanna stay together anymore let me take a deep breath babe if you need me. me and neil'll be hangin' out with the DREAM KING Neil says hi by the way I don't believe you're leaving cause me and Charles Manson like the same ice cream I think it's that girl and I think there're pieces of me you've never seen maybe she's just pieces of me you've never seen well *all the world is all I am the black of the blackest ocean and that tear in your hand all the world is DANGLIN'.. . danglin'. . . danglin' for me DARLIN' you don't know the power that you have with that tear in your hand tear in your hand* maybe I ain't used to maybes smashing in a cold room cutting my hands up every time I touch you maybe maybe it's time to wave goodbye now caught a ride with the moon I know I know you well well better than I used to HAZE all clouded up my mind in the DAZE of the why it could've never been so you say and I say you know you're full of wish and your "baby baby baby babies" I tell you there're pieces of me you've never seen maybe she's just pieces of me you've never seen well

Thoughts

right now I picked up a
magazine ooh here we go fifteen hundred years fifteen hundred years
right here burning witches burning
books burning babies in their LOOKS
yes indeed burning everything that's
sacred in my jeans yeah yeah
thoughts right now she's been everybody else's girl thoughts right now
right thoughts right now right right
now am I here am I here I'm never
here I'm never here I'm NEVER here
I'm never here never a bird or a
FLOWER in the tree or the pain of
the respect there of yes indeed
thoughts right now what will become
of me become of her become of we

TOODLES MR. JIM

toodles Mr. Jim
you cherry picker
toodles
I say, so long
hear that your grave's a little warm, you stickler
sing 'em all your happy song
it's today
today Sunday
by your grave

I say toodles Mr. Jim
you cherry picker
taught me so well
how to spell
those red hm. And. Hey.
you know she deserved that nose
splattered and swattered blood in my hands
not a nice day for your little girl
but you came to my aid instead

but now it's toodles Mr. Jim
you cherry picker
build that ladder well
teach me just where those boys can climb
when they've got a spell

toodles Mr. Jim
you are my sweet,
favourite neighbor of them all let them
girls go to their parties
I don't care
'cause I'm with you. Still.

TWINKLE

sure that star can twinkle
and you're watching it do
boy so hard boy so hard
but I know a girl
twice as hard
and I'm sure
said I'm sure
she's watching it too
no matter what tie she's got in her right
dresser
tied
I know she's watching that star

gonna twinkle
gonna twinkle
gonna twinkle

and last time I knew
she worked at an Abbey in Iona
she said "I killed a man T
I've gotta stay hidden in this Abbey"
but I can see that star
when she twinkles
and she twinkles
and I sure can
that means
I sure can

that means
I sure can
so hard
so hard

Upside Down

god I love to turn my little blue world upside down god I love to turn my little blue world upside down inside my head the noise chatter chatter CHATTER chatter chatter you see I'm afraid I'll always be still comin' out of my mother upside down Don't you love to turn this little blue girl upside down oh I know you love to turn this little blue girl baby upside down but my heart it says you've been shatter shatter shatter SHATTER shattered and I know you're still a boy still comin' out of your mother but when you gonna stand on your own I say the world is sick you say tell me what that makes us darlin' you see you always find my faults faster than you find your own you say the world is getting rid of her DEMONS I say baby what have you been smokin' well I dreamed I dreamed I dreamed I loved a black boy my daddy would scream oh yeah don't you love to turn this little blue girl upside any kind of touch I think is better than none even upside down but you see I'm tangled up got a kitten kitten kitten KITTEN in my air Cincinnati I like the word it's the only thing we can't seem to turn upside down well I found the secret to life I'm O.K. when everything is not O.K.

The Waitress

So I want to kill this waitress She's worked here a year longer than I If I did it fast you know that's an act of kindness

But I believe in peace I believe in peace Bitch I believe in peace

I want to kill this waitress I can't believe this violence in mind and is her power all in her club sandwich

I want to kill this killing wish they're too many stars and not enough sky Boys all think she's living kindness ask a fellow waitress ask a fellow waitress

Way Down

maybe I'm the afterglow
'cause I'm with the band you know
don't you hear the laughter
on the way down
yes I am the anchorman
dining here with Son of Sam
a hair too much to chat of
on the way down
gonna meet a great big star
gonna drive his great big car
gonna have it all here
on the way down
the way down
the way down
she knows
let's go
way down
way down
the way down
she knows

THE WRONG BAND

I think it's perfectly clear we're in the wrong band Ginger is always sincere just not to one man she called me up and she said you know that I'm drowning it's the dog trainer again he says that he thinks that she needs more hands

I think it perfectly clear we're in the wrong band Senator let's be sincere as much as you can he called her up and he said the new prosecutor soon will be wanting a word so she's got a soft spot for heels and spurs and there's something believin in her voice again said there's something believin instead of just leavin

And she gets her cigars from the sweet fat man I think it's perfectly clear we're in the wrong band Heidi says she'll be sincere as much as she can I called her up and I said you know that I'm drowning put on your raincoat again cause even the sun's got a price on it and there's something believin in her voice again said there's something believin instead of just leavin

She said it's time I open my eyes don't be afraid to open your eyes maybe she's right maybe she's right maybe she's right maybe she's right

Winter

snow can wait I forgot my mittens wipe my
nose get my new boots on I get a little warm in my
heart when I think of winter I put my hand in my
father's glove I run off where the DRIFTS GET
DEEPER sleeping beauty trips me with a frown I
hear a voice "you must learn to stand up for yourself
cause I can't always be around" *he says when you
gonna make up your mind when you gonna love you
as much as I do when you gonna make up your mind
cause things are gonna CHANGE so fast all the white
horses are still in bed I tell you that I'll always want
you near you say that things change my dear* boys get
discovered as winter MELTS flowers competing for
the sun years go by and I'm here still waiting wither-
ing where some snowman was mirror mirror where's
the crystal palace but I can only see myself SKATING
around the truth who I am but I know dad the ice is
getting thin hair is grey and the fires are burning so
many dreams on the shelf you say I wanted you to be
PROUD of me I always wanted that myself he says
when you gonna make up your mind when you gonna
love you as much as I do when you gonna make up
your mind cause things change so fast all the WHITE
HORSES have gone ahead I tell you that I always
want you near you say that things change my dear

Yes, Anastasia

I know what you want the magpies have come if you know me so well then tell me
which hand I use

Make them go make it go

Saw her there in a restaurant Poppy don't go I know your mother is a good one
but Poppy don't go I'll take you home show me the things I've been missin
show me the ways I forgot to be speaking show me the ways to get back to the garden
show me the ways to get around the get around show me the ways to button up
buttons that have forgotten they're buttons well we can't have that forgetting that

girls girls what have we done to ourselves driving on the vine over clothes lines
but officer I saw the sign thought I'd been through this in 1919 counting the
tears of ten thousand men and gathered them all but my feet are slipping there's
something we left on the windowsill there's something we left yes

We'll see how brave you are we'll see how fast you'll be running we'll see how
brave you are yes, Anastasia and all your dollies have friends

Thought she deserved no less than she'd give well happy birthday her blood's on
my hands it's kind of a shame cause I did like that dress it's funny the things that
you find in the rain the things that you find in the mall in the date-mines in the
knot still in her hair on the bus I'm on my way down all the girls seem to be there

Come along now little darlin' come along now with me come along now little
darlin' we'll see how brave you are